STORM

For Ben

A TEMPLAR BOOK

First published in the UK in 2018 by Templar Publishing,
an imprint of King's Road Publishing,
part of the Bonnier Publishing Group,
The Plaza, 535 King's Road, London, SW10 0SZ
www.templarco.co.uk
www.bonnierpublishing.com

1 3 5 7 9 10 8 6 4 2

ISBN 978-1-78741-075-6 (Hardback)
ISBN 978-1-78741-242-2 (Paperback)

Designed by Genevieve Webster
Edited by Alison Ritchie

Printed in Malaysia

Sam Usher

STORM

templar
books

When I woke up
this morning,
the wind was rattling
the windows.

I couldn't wait to
go outside.

I said, "Grandad! We could do kicking up the leaves,

swooping and flying

and leaning in the wind."

Grandad said, "It's the perfect day to fly the kite!
But we'll have to find it first . . ."

Outside the wind blustered and blew.

We looked for the kite in the cupboard.

I said, "Grandad, it's your cricket bat!
I remember this!"

Grandad said,
"So do I!"

But we didn't find the kite.

And the wind huffed and howled.

So we looked in the study.

I said, "Remember when you let me post that important letter?"

Grandad said,
"Ah, yes, so I did –
we went by boat."

And the wind whistled and whooshed.

But we still hadn't found the kite.
So we looked under the stairs and I said,
"Grandad, it's your telescope!
Do you remember our expedition?"

Grandad said, "Yes, we went into the secret cave,
and had that perfect picnic!"

We kept on searching.
We thought we'd never
find the kite.

Then I shouted, "Grandad! Look!

And Grandad said, "YES! You've found it!"

We were off to the park at last!

The kite flew first time.

Grandad said, "Hold on tight!"

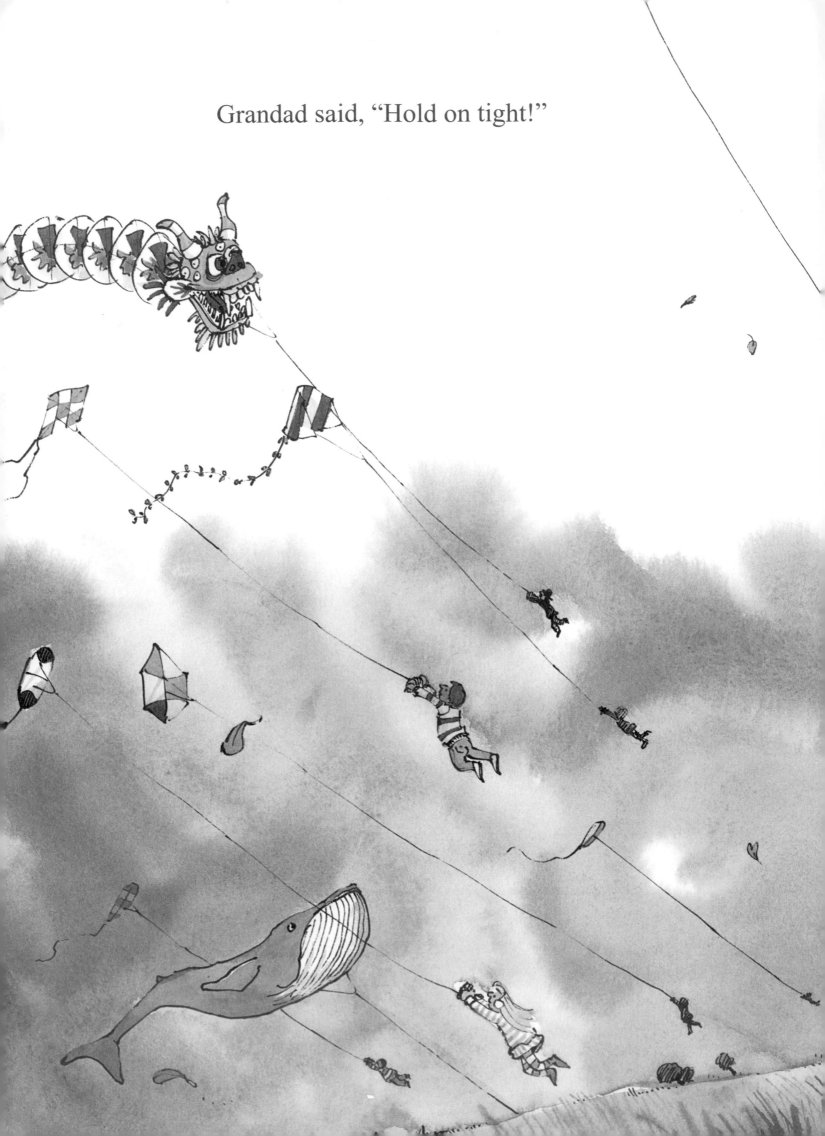

We did
swooping and
flying.

Then I let go!

But Grandad
caught it.

He said,
"There's a storm brewing!
Let's head for home."

We prepared for landing.

Back at home,
Grandad said,
"The best adventure
is an adventure
shared."

And I agreed.

I hope it's stormy
again tomorrow.